Treatise on Elegant Living

Honoré de Balzac, after the daguerreotype
by Louis-Auguste Bisson, 1842.

Treatise on Elegant Living

Honoré de Balzac

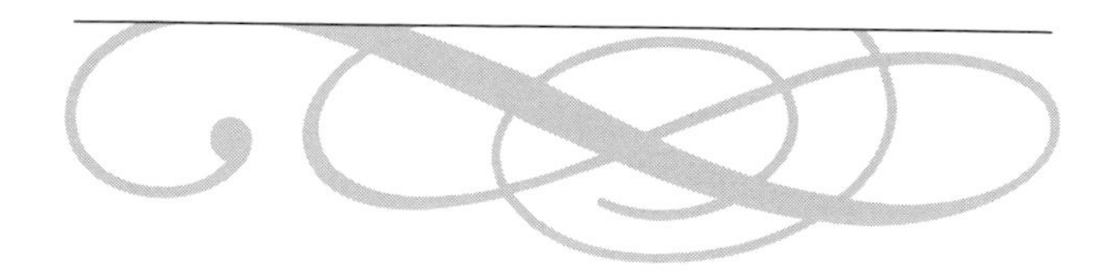

Translated by Napoleon Jeffries

WAKEFIELD PRESS, CAMBRIDGE, MASSACHUSETTS

Wakefield Press, P.O. Box 425645, Cambridge, MA 02142

This book was set in Garamond Premier Pro by Wakefield Press. Printed and bound in the United States of America.

ISBN: 978-0-9841155-0-1

Available through D.A.P./Distributed Art Publishers
155 Sixth Avenue, 2nd Floor
New York, New York 10013
Tel: (212) 627-1999
Fax: (212) 627-9484

10 9 8 7 6 5 4 3 2

Contents

TRANSLATOR'S INTRODUCTION

"Giving style" to one's character—a great and rare art! It is exercised by those who see all the strengths and weaknesses of their own natures and then comprehend them in an artistic plan until everything appears as art and reason and even weakness delights the eye. . . .

—Friedrich Nietzsche

AS LONG AS CLOTHES make the man, the dandy will continue to cast his shadow into the twenty-first century. He may at times seem like a pale shadow, an outline without actual content—the ghost of an apparition of a man: superficiality remains, after all, one of the more superficial attributes ascribed to the dandy. But in an age when history and heritage are fading, where appearances are looked upon as deceiving while also accepted as truth, and where rebellion and conformity exchange masks, the legacy of the dandy remains illuminating. Given high capitalism's reduction of being to having, there is even a sort of salvational aura to this figure of the dandy, who two centuries ago broke down the barriers between aesthetics and the everyday, renounced the "busy life" of production and utility, and instead turned his own life into a work of art.

What *was* the dandy, though? If the dandy denies predecessors, and pointedly leaves no progeny, he does nonetheless have a history, and Honoré de Balzac may be credited as one of the first to have made a conscious attempt to imagine this history. Its starting point is incontestable: be he fop, urban narcissist, metrosexual, or artist formerly known as Prince, every dandy bears allegiance to Beau Brummell, the original dandy—the *only* dandy, perhaps, that ever truly existed. For Brummell left no model to emulate, no handbook to follow, no anecdotes to relate, and no real clues for posterity to understand what had made him who he was—what had prompted Lord Byron to claim that he would have rather been Brummell than Napoleon. Even when alive, Brummell was more of an abstraction than a man, and with his absence, dandyism necessarily became as much a theory as a practice, and the man as much a literary figure as a historical one. Brummell has become an ineffable archetype; if he does not have quite the same literary stature of Don Juan or Hamlet, he could still easily rub shoulders with the likes of Oblomov or Sherlock Holmes (if, that is, rubbing shoulders were not an activity he abhorred).

Born in 1778, George Bryan Brummell reigned over the early nineteenth century in England and the rather contemptible period of the British Regency: exclusivism held sway, a reactionary idleness filled in for a crumbling aristocracy, and the unspoken rules for initiates able to afford the game were established not so much by George IV, but by his rebellious favorite. Brummell was, as Barbey d'Aurevilly put it, the "autocrat of opinion." The measuring rod for every action (and more significantly, every nonaction), was fashionability: marriage and women were not fashionable; going into debt and being idle were. It is hard not to side with Thomas Carlyle in his declaration of what was essentially class war against that exclusive minority—a war he described as being between the Dandies and the "Drudges."

What would have been a fairly clear-cut class antagonism, however, was complicated by Brummell's background: for if he acted the aristocrat, lived the life of an aristocrat, and was courted by the aristocracy, Brummell was no aristocrat. He was a new kind of autocrat, natural-born in that he came from no family (to his middle-class family's understandable chagrin), and sired none; he was for all intents and purposes a self-sired autocrat, whose example in dignified manners, elegant dress, and stoic distinction could eventually be followed by members of any class and occupation—provided, of course, they had access to a sufficient amount of funds to maintain a life of leisure.

But Brummell was more than an infiltrator of ranks; he was a new kind of *individual*. If it was his nature to live beyond his means (insolvency was the inevitable outcome for Brummell and his followers), it was his legacy to live beyond society's understanding. Whereas the snob (a different character altogether, albeit one understandably confused with the Regency dandies) maneuvered within society by laws and manners established by that society, the dandy operated in accordance with laws of his own making, and for an audience that consisted of himself before anyone. The practice of elegance and taste was one that either passed unnoticed by anyone save the initiate, or one that shocked the populace; it could find an outlet in the reactionary politics of the secret society, or the more striking and rebellious form of modernist shock: the dandies were the first to employ the now normalized practice of shocking the bourgeoisie.

It took the French, however, to recognize and elaborate upon these still budding qualities of the dandy, and formulate an intellectual brand of aesthetic and social egoism that would inform modernism and would find its culmination in the figure of Charles Baudelaire. It would be in France that the dandy and the bohemian would become two sides of the same coin, the dandy simply having money, the bohemian doing without (it was even quite natural to start a dandy, as Baudelaire did, and finish a bohemian). And it is in France that the second, and most interesting, stage of dandyism took place.

There were three broad phases of dandyism: the social dandyism of Beau Brummell and the early nineteenth-century Regency; the French intellectual dandyism of the mid-century; and what has become the more widely known commercial dandyism (what Ellen Moers referred to as "hedonistic dandyism") of Oscar Wilde and the fin-de-siècle, a basically British chapter that in a roundabout way took its cue from the French rather than the British Regency. It was a somewhat muddled cue, though, blending dandyism with the decadent movement that had since taken shape, resulting in the amalgamated "aesthete" who bore but faint resemblance to the original puritanical mold of Brummell.

The French themselves took a muddled cue from the Regency dandy, though, partly owing to a strong early nineteenth-century Anglomania in France that, as Moers put it, "made the dandy and the romantic one and the same, though the two had scarcely met at home."[1] The combination would prove to be productive, however, and it helped turn the French dandy into a crucial transitional figure between the late eighteenth-century libertine and the late nineteenth-century decadent.[2] Moers described the dandy as being the "epitome of selfish irresponsibility . . . ideally free of all human commitments that conflict with taste: passions, moralities, ambitions, politics or occupations."[3] By exchanging the words "taste" and "passions" over the colon dividing them in this definition, though, one could essentially change this definition of the dandy to that of the libertine who preceded him.

This simple exchange of taste for passion, though, made for a world of pointed contrast between the two autocrats: if the libertine embraced his nature and pursued sexual pleasure by mastering others, the dandy denied his nature, mastered himself, and displayed what Barbey d'Aurevilly described as an "antique calm" and an "undecidedly intellectual sex." If marriage and reproduction were both anathema to libertine and dandy, their reasons were opposite: for the libertine, they interfered with his private pleasures, while for the dandy, they interfered with his social persona. Whereas the libertine took an Enlightenment zest in vulgarity and blasphemy in the boudoir, the dandy, as impertinent as he may have been in the salon, could never be accused of vulgarity. If the libertine parleyed with invective and violence behind closed doors, the dandy's weapon of choice was his social use of wit; if the libertine indulged in cruelty by stabbing his victims with pins and daggers, the dandy's finest stabs were always the cut of his suit and the cutting remarks he reserved for friends and enemies alike. If the libertine removed his societal mask within the boudoir in order to drink in a victim's blood, the dandy did the opposite: "These Stoics of the boudoir drink their own blood under their mask and remain masked."[4]

As Barbey d'Aurevilly concluded: "Passion is too true to be dandyesque." But this opposition of nature and artifice actually points to the essential, common feature between Sade's libertine and the dandy: their shared opposition to Jean-Jacques Rousseau's Romantic belief in the noble savage, the belief that man is essentially good when in a state of nature. Both libertine and dandy considered cruelty to be most natural, virtue an artificial construct, and egoism the only law worth obeying. But the dandy differed from the libertine in that he did not embrace this conception of the natural state, and instead chose to celebrate the excesses of artifice. When Baudelaire (in many ways Sade's truest disciple) posited virtue and beauty as artificial constructs, his adoption of the dandy's role and embracement of artifice ultimately turned him into something of a dark moralist.

It is also on this point that the French dandy signaled a significant break from both Romantic and libertine, both of whom, despite their opposing outlooks on nature, ultimately aimed at an absorption into nature, a loss of the self via the frenzied throes of natural or sexual carnage. This quest for self-dissipation would find its echo in the decadent, whose apposite, almost Romantic, withdrawal into artifice turned him into not just an antihero, but even a nonhero. The dandy, on the other hand, though he shunned nature, only *used* artifice and remained utterly dependant on society. Without an observer, he was like the sound made by George Berkeley's tree falling unobserved in a wood: he would in effect cease to exist. As long as he had an audience, the dandy relinquished his self-identity to no one: self-control, dignity, and pride yielded nothing to emotion; paradox battled against any manner of conformity; and death itself, far from holding any dark attraction, was merely something that happened to other people. Nature has no heroes, and artifice consumes them; it was the middle ground of dandyism that made it, as Baudelaire put it, "the last spark of heroism amid decadence."[5]

This new heroic formulation of the dandy would be established by three essential and defining texts of French dandyism, all composed by exceptional men who were themselves significant and very personalized embodiments of dandyism: Jules Barbey d'Aurevilly's 1845 *On Dandyism and George Brummell*, Charles Baudelaire's 1863 cornerstone to modernism *The Painter of Modern Life*, and the treatise that helped pave the way for both them, Honoré de Balzac's 1830 *Treatise on Elegant Living*.

Balzac's *Treatise* stands at the threshold of French dandyism, marking a historical and theoretical shift that would either influence or herald the dandyism to come.[6] Although intellectual dandyism is often considered to stem from Barbey d'Aurevilly's classic work on Brummell, Balzac was the first to open the door. He wrote his treatise only a few months after George IV's death, a death that officially signaled the end of Regency exclusivism, and thereby the end of Regency dandyism. It is significant that this end was directly followed by the beginnings of French dandyism, whose groundwork Balzac was helping to establish.

Even those familiar with Balzac's novels, however, may be initially taken off guard by the notion of that giant presenting himself as an expert on elegance—let alone a self-proclaimed originator of, to use his own coinage, the new science of "elegantology." Even more surprising may be the fact that Balzac considered himself something of a practitioner of the science. He was an odd manifestation of early French dandyism: taking his cues in dress from friends such as Eugène Sue and Lautour-Mézeray (both of whom make appearances in this treatise), Balzac proved to be more of a part-time dandy. The dandy memorialist Captain Gronow provided a particularly amusing assessment of the man's elegance in practice: "The great enchanter was one of the oiliest and commonest looking mortals I ever beheld; being short and corpulent, with a broad florid face, a cascade of double chins, and straight greasy hair . . . [he] dressed in the worst possible taste, wore sparkling jewels on a dirty shirt front, and diamond rings on unwashed fingers. . . ."[7]

Balzac did not, obviously, quite match up to the exacting standards he established in his treatise, and in the end, he himself probably did not see himself in the category. But he introduced a new category into the system, one placed squarely between the busy life and the elegant life: the *thinking* life of the artist. In Balzac's words: "The artist is an exception: his idleness is work, and his work, repose; he is elegant and slovenly in turn; he dons, as he pleases, the plowman's overalls, and determines the tails worn by the man in fashion; he is not subject to laws: he imposes them."

This introduction of the category of artist would have lasting repercussions on dandyism, particularly the later dandyism of Baudelaire, who had no interest whatsoever in aristocracy, and who essentially presented himself to, and performed for (and ultimately rejected), the artist community. The category of artist is also what shapes Balzac's portrayal of Brummell. Like most of his contemporaries, and despite Brummell's presence in France (where he spent his last years in exile to escape his creditors), Balzac's actual knowledge and understanding of the real Beau Brummell was superficial at best. The abstract nature of the *figure* of Brummell in France is illustrated by the fact that his very name was consistently misspelled (Balzac employed the spelling of "Brummel" that was standard in France at the time, but this has been adjusted for this translation). Barbey d'Aurevilly would later undertake his biographical portrait of Brummell without even knowing whether or not his subject had ever married; his portrait of the dandy was composed of carefully selected biographical facts which he assembled to create the personalized dandy he envisioned, rather than the dandy that had lived. It must be noted, then, that even though it had been written when Brummell was still alive, the Brummell who appears in Balzac's treatise is pure fiction and inaccurate in a number of details (a few of which have been pointed out in the notes). What Balzac has him say, however, does the dandy justice. After poking some fun at the inevitable ravages of time upon the dandy (imagining a certain degree of portliness and a wig, details that fall short of the very depressing poverty and madness that in fact awaited Brummell in his final years), Balzac proceeds to envision him as the theorist, aphorist, and author that he never was in life. It is this effort that distinguishes Balzac's approach to his subject, and it is a difference in evidence from his opening epigraph by Virgil: *Mens agitat molem* (Mind moves matter). If the effective and often accurate metaphor employed by the English anti-dandiacals described the dandy as an empty suit of clothes, Balzac here pointedly puts the man back into the suit. It is this shift that leads him to make what may at first be a surprising assertion midway through his treatise that the dandy is a "heresy of elegant living." This dandy he refutes, though, is the dandy of the Regency, the dandy that is to be supplanted by the dandy he is heralding. The snobbery of two-dimensional dandyism was past, the dandy of gender and sexual politics was yet to come; this redefined dandyism, rooted in a redefined Brummell, was the dandyism of ambiguous tyranny, cynical defiance, reactionary rebellion, and budding modernism.

This new dandy also tempers Balzac's essay, which can at times read fairly conservatively considering the July

Revolution that had taken place in France just a few months earlier. Throughout all of his stages, the dandy was very much a product of his times, and if the Regency gave rise to his first incarnation, the political backdrop in France set the tone for a more overt democratization of dandyism, and opened the discourse to the broader political and sociological question of leisure time that would become an increasingly prominent topic over the coming decades.[8] For Balzac's conflation of dandy and artist echoes the one then taking place between the aristocracy and the middle class, the two of which, he here declares, shall "lead the people onto the path of civilization and light."

July Revolution or not, this alignment was obviously not going to change much for "the people," and Balzac's obvious cynicism in this treatise leaves Carlyle's Drudges little else to do but continue drudging along. But the "enlargened caste" ruling over them, Balzac's conjoining of "natural-born" aristocratic elegance with the educated middle-class arts and sciences, echoes the paradoxical foundation to this treatise; for if, as Balzac declares, "elegance is less an art than a feeling," if any man can get rich but must be "born elegant" to be elegant, then of what use is a handbook on the subject? The contradiction in the attempt to democratize a way of living that cannot be taught or studied is one that inevitably arises throughout much of the literature on dandyism.[9] It is also what makes the French dandy such a complicated figure, a seamless mixture of reactionary conservatism and avant-garde revolution masked by an unnervingly calm exterior. This contradiction would find itself resolved only in practice: Barbey d'Aurevilly would embrace right-wing conservatism, whereas Baudelaire played a minor role in the 1848 Revolution. By the end of the century, a good portion of the Bohemian Parisian avant-garde would emerge from the shadows of dandyism and decadence to choose between the extremist paths of conservative proto-fascism and bomb-throwing anarchism.

Balzac maintains (perhaps masks) the paradox at the root of his subject with the folksy-scientific style of the physiology that was popular in his day, and one that he repeatedly employed—most fully in his *Physiology of Marriage*, but less blatantly throughout all of his novels. All physiologies of that time stemmed from the work of Johann Caspar Lavater, which in its broad strokes offered the sometimes troubling, and decidedly flawed, lesson that appearances were, in fact, everything.[10] But Balzac's more immediate mentor in the format was Jean Anthelme Brillat-Savarin, whose 1825 *Physiology of Taste* injected a range of humor, anecdotes, and axioms into an extremely personalized and popularized version of the scientific framework. What Brillat-Savarin had done for gourmandism and gastronomy, Balzac had intended to do for nineteenth-century French society. His *Human Comedy* would go a long way in carrying out this project, although its 91 novels and short stories fell short of the 137 he had originally planned. An essential component to his project, however, was to be a series of analytical studies to be entitled *Pathology of Social Life*. Only the first part, *The Physiology of Marriage*, was ever written, though, and it has long been available in English translation. Two of the others, the *Anatomy of Educational Bodies* and the *Monograph on Virtue*, were never written. The fourth, which he referred to variously as *Complete Treatise on Exterior Life*, *On Elegant Living*, or the *Pathology of Social Life* itself, was at least started. Though it had originally been written for the journal *La Mode*, it was his intention to incorporate the *Treatise on Elegant Living* into it, along with two other completed components, his *Theory of Walking* and *Treatise on Modern Stimulants.* A number of other short essays and sketches exist that may well have been intended for eventual inclusion in this project (titles include "Physiology of the Cigar," "Gastronomic Physiology," "Physiology of Clothing," and "Study of Manners through Gloves"), but given Balzac's voluminous output and lack of specific indications, only guesses can be made as to what would or would not have been incorporated.

It is obvious, given the outline Balzac sketched out at the end of chapter III, that the *Treatise on Elegant Living* was never finished. It is also likely that the later *Theory of Walking* grew out of the projected chapter on gait and deportment, but nothing exists of those chapters he announces on manners and conversation, nor of what was to be the intriguing contribution by Eugène Sue on impertinence. Be that as it may, Balzac did set enough down to allow us a clear understanding of the unified triad essential to any understanding and practice of elegant living: simplicity, cleanliness, and harmony. Whether taking it as an illuminating cornerstone to his *Human Comedy*, a crucial chapter in the history of dandyism, or as an entertaining handbook on the use and power derived from perfecting one's outer appearance, the reader should find this short work amply rewarding.

* * *

The translator would like to thank Judy Feldmann and Inez Hedges for helping to make this translation better than it would have been, and Emily Gutheinz for rendering it into such an elegant form. Any flaws to be found in this text may be ascribed to the translator.

NOTES

1. Ellen Moers, *The Dandy: Brummell to Beerbohm* (New York: Viking Press, 1960), p. 121. This study remains, to my knowledge, the best historical overview of dandyism in any language, and the one that has most influenced my understanding of the subject.

2. Two figures most effectively and clearly represented in the works of the Marquis de Sade and J.-K. Huysmans, respectively. The libertine finds his archetype in the character of Dolmancé in Sade's *Philosophy in the Bedroom*, the decadent in that of Des Esseintes in Huysmans's *Against the Grain*.

3. Moers, *The Dandy*, p. 13.

4. Babrey d'Aurevilly, *Dandyism*, tr. Douglas Airslie (New York: PAJ Publishing Company, 1988), p. 64.

5. Baudelaire, *The Painter of Modern Life and Other Essays* (New York: Phaidon, 1964), p. 28.

6. This shift is nowhere better illustrated than in maxim XXXIX of this treatise, Balzac's direct denunciation of dandyism. Though there is a bit of an anxiety of influence in his labeling of dandyism as a "heresy," Balzac's denunciation is also what serves as the groundwork to the redefined dandyism of Barbey d'Aurevilly and Baudelaire.

7. Quoted in Moers, *The Dandy*, p. 129.

8. As paradoxical as the concept may seem, one could see something of a "democratic dandyism" in a work like the 1883 polemic, *The Right to Be Lazy*, by Karl Marx's son-in-law, Paul Lafargue.

9. It is the same contradiction that arises with a number of related philosophies: it is impossible to envision, for example, a society of overmen in Nietzsche's philosophy, or a society of libertines in Sade's dark and inverted utopia.

10. It was Lavater who gave rise to the influential pseudoscience of phrenology that was still considered legitimate when Balzac was writing this treatise, and that would not be officially debunked until several years later in the late 1830s. Its influence, however, would continue well beyond that.

First Part: Generalities

Mens agitat molem.
VIRGIL

A man's mind can be known by the
manner in which he carries his walking stick.
FASHIONABLE TRANSLATION

First Chapter: Prolegomena

Civilization has distributed men among three basic types . . . It would have been easy for us to have colored in these categories the way M. Charles Dupin does;[1] but since charlatanism would go against the grain of a work of Christian philosophy, we shall refrain from mixing painting with the x of algebra, and endeavor, by stating the most secret tenets of elegant living, to be understood even by our antagonists: those in turned-down boots.

Modern customs have created three classes of beings:

The man who works;
The man who thinks;
The man who does nothing.

From this we get three fairly complete formulas that can express any type of life, from the poetic and restless novel of the *bohemian* to the dreary and soporific history book of constitutional kings:

The busy life;
The artist's life;
The elegant life.

§ 1—On the Busy Life

There are no variants on the theme of the busy life. By working with his ten fingers, man renounces his destiny; he becomes a means, and despite all our philanthropy, the results alone win our admiration. Everywhere man goes swooning before some piles of stones, and if he remembers those who piled them up, it is only to shower pity on them; if he appreciates the grand design of the architect, he deems that his workers are nothing more than human winches, interchangeable with wheelbarrows, shovels, and pickaxes.

Is this an injustice? No. Like steam engines, men enlisted by work all appear the same, with nothing individual about them. The man-instrument is a sort of social zero, and no matter how many of them there are, they will never form a sum unless preceded by some numerals.

A plowman, a bricklayer, a soldier: these are all uniform fragments of the same mass, the same tool whose handle alone differs. They go to bed and get up with the sun; some at cockcrow; others, at reveille; this one, an old army man, gets two ells of blue woolen cloth and boots; that one gets whatever rags happen to be lying around; all get the coarsest food: beating plaster or beating men, harvesting beans or strokes of the sword, such is, in every season, the text of their efforts. Work seems to be a riddle whose answer they seek until their dying day. All too often the sad *pensum* of their existence is rewarded by the acquisition of a little wooden bench on which they sit at the door of a thatched cottage, under a dusty elder tree, without having to fear some lackey telling them:

"Get a move on, old man! We only give to the poor on Mondays."

For all these poor wretches, life is summed up by *bread in the bin*, and elegance by a chest of worn clothes.

The small retail dealer, the second lieutenant, the assistant editor: these are less degraded examples of the busy life, but their existence is still marked by vulgarity. It is still work, still the winch: only the mechanism is a little more intricate, and the intellect meshes with it parsimoniously.

Far from being an artist, the tailor always, to the minds of these people, takes on the form of a pitiless bill: they abuse the institution of detachable collars, reproach themselves for an extravagance as being a theft from their creditors, and for them, a carriage is a hackney cab in normal circumstances, a hired carriage for funerals and weddings.

If they don't hoard money like tacticians in order to assure bed and board in their old age, the hope of their bee's life barely goes any further than that: the possession of a very cold room on the fifth floor, rue Boucherat;[2] then a bonnet and percale gloves for the woman; a gray hat and a demitasse for the husband; a Saint-Denis education[3] and a partial scholarship for the children; *boiled meat* with parsley twice a week for everyone. Not quite zeros and not altogether numerals, these creatures are perhaps decimals.

In this *doleful* city,[4] life is resolved by a pension or some unearned income on the ledger, and elegance by draperies with fringes, a *lit en bateau*, and candlesticks under glass.

If we climb a few more rungs up the social ladder, on which busy men clamber and sway like ship's boys in the rigging of a large vessel, we find the doctor, the priest, the attorney, the lawyer, the petty magistrate, the wholesaler, the local squire, the bureaucrat, the field officer, etc. These characters are marvelously sophisticated appliances, whose pumps, chains, balance wheels—all of their gearwheels, in fact—all carefully polished, adjusted, and oiled, perform their revolutions in respectable and elaborate caparisons. But this life is always a life of movement in which thoughts are still neither free nor very fruitful. Every day these messieurs have to perform a certain number of revolutions written down in *agendas.* These little books take the place of the *yard dogs*[5] that harassed them at school not so long ago, and remind them that at any time of the day they are slaves to a being of reason a thousand times more temperamental and ungrateful than a sovereign.

By the time they reach the age of rest, the sense of *fashion* has been obliterated and the time of elegance has slipped away, never to return. Consequently the carriage that takes them around has a projecting running board with a variety of purposes, or is decrepit like that of the famous Portal.[6] With them, the prejudice for cashmere lives on; their wives wear diamond rivières and girandoles of jewels; their luxury is always an investment; in their homes, everything is *well-to-do*, and you read above the theater box: "Speak to the attendant." If they count as numerals in the social circle, then they are single digits.

For the *parvenus* of this class, life is resolved by the title of baron, and elegance by a large, well-plumed footman, or by a box seat at the Feydeau.[7]

There ends the busy life. The high-ranking civil servant, the prelate, the general, the great landowner, the member of the cabinet, the valet,* and princes fall in the category of people of leisure and belong to the elegant life.

* The valet is a kind of luggage essential to elegant living.

After finishing this sad autopsy of the social body, a philosopher feels such disgust for the prejudices that induce men to pass by one another, avoiding each other like snakes in the grass, that he needs to tell himself: "I take no perverse delight in building a nation, I accept it as it is . . ."

This general survey of society, taken *en masse*, will help us conceive our first aphorisms, which we formulate as such:

APHORISMS

I

The goal of the civilized man as of the savage is repose.

II

Absolute repose produces spleen.

III

Elegant living is, in the broad acceptance of the term, the art of animating repose.

IV

The man accustomed to work cannot understand elegant living.

V

CoROLLARY. *To be fashionable, one must enjoy repose without undergoing work: in other words, one must get the four winning numbers in a lottery, be the son of a millionaire, prince, sinecurist, or a holder of several remunerative positions.*

§ II—On the Artist's Life

The artist is an exception: his idleness is work, and his work, repose; he is elegant and slovenly in turn; he dons, as he pleases, the plowman's overalls, and determines the tails worn by the man in fashion; he is not subject to laws: he imposes them. Whether he occupies himself by doing nothing, or ponders over a masterpiece without appearing busy; whether he leads a horse with a wooden bit or leads with long reins the four horses of a *britschka*;[8] whether he lacks even twenty-five cents or throws around handfuls of gold—he is always the expression of a great thought and towers over society.

When M. Peel entered the home of the viscount Chateaubriand,[9] he found himself in a study in which all the furniture was oak: the secretary, a millionaire thirty times over, suddenly saw the massive gold and silver furnishings that were cluttering up England crushed by this simplicity.

The artist is always great. He has an elegance and a life all his own, because everything about him mirrors his intelligence and his glory. There are as many lives characterized by new ideas as there are artists. With them, fashion must not be forced: these uncontrolled beings fashion everything as they please. If they take possession of a pile of money, it is in order to transform it.

From this doctrine a European aphorism can be inferred:

VI

An artist lives as he wishes, or . . . as he can.

§ III—On the Elegant Life

If we neglected to define elegant living here, this treatise would be crippled. A treatise without definition is like a colonel with two legs amputated: it can barely hobble along. To define is to abridge: let us, then, abridge.

Elegant living is the perfection of outer and material life;

Or:

The art of spending one's income as a man of wit;

Or even:

The science that teaches us to do nothing like anyone else, while appearing to do everything just like them;

But perhaps even better:

The development of grace and taste in everything that belongs to us and that surrounds us;

Or more logically:

Knowing how to honor oneself with one's fortune.

According to our worthy friend, E. de G . . . ,[10] this would be:

Nobility conveyed into things.

According to T.-P. Smith:[11]

Elegant living is the fertilizing principle of industriousness.

As M. Jacotot has it, a treatise on elegant living is pointless since it can be found in its entirety in *Telemachus*. (See the Salente Constitution.)[12]

To understand M. Cousin,[13] it would be, in a more elevated way of thinking:

"The exercise of reason, necessarily accompanied by that of the senses, the imagination, and the heart, which, combining with the primitive institutions, with the direct illuminations of animalism, dyes life with its colors." (See page 44 of the *Cours de l'histoire de la Philosophie*, if the phrase *elegant living* is not actually the answer to this rebus.)

In the doctrine of Saint-Simon:

Elegant living would be the greatest illness to afflict a society that started from this principle: "A great fortune is a theft."

As Chodruc[14] has it:

It is a tissue of trifles and nonsense.

Elegant living indeed comprises all of these subsidiary definitions, circumlocutions of our aphorism III; but in our opinion, it involves even more important questions, and to remain faithful to our system of abbreviation we shall attempt to develop them.

A nation of wealthy people is a political dream that is impossible to realize. A nation is necessarily made up of people who produce and people who consume. How is it that the one who sows, plants, waters, and harvests is precisely the one who eats the least? This result is a mystery easy enough to uncover, but one that many people like to look upon as a grand providential thought. We shall perhaps provide an explanation for it later on, when we reach the end of the path taken by humanity. For the time being, at the risk of being accused of aristocracy, we will say quite candidly that a man placed on the last rung of society has no more right to ask God for an explanation for his fate than does an oyster.

This remark, at once philosophical and Christian, shall no doubt settle the question in the eyes of people who spend some time poring over the constitutional charters, and as we are not speaking to anyone else, we will continue.

For as long as societies have existed, a government has always by necessity been an insurance policy for the rich against the poor. The domestic struggle generated by this alleged distribution *à la Montgomery* kindles a general passion for *fortune* among civilized men, an expression that prototypes all particular ambitions; because from this desire to not belong to the suffering and persecuted class stems the nobility, the aristocracy, distinctions, courtiers, courtesans, etc.

But this type of fever that leads man to see greasy poles everywhere and to feel distressed over being perched only a quarter, a third, or halfway up, has inevitably engendered excessive pride and vanity. Given that vanity is nothing but the art of putting on one's Sunday best all the time, every man felt the need to have, as an example of his power, a loaded sign to inform the passersby of where he was perching on the great greasy pole, at the top of which the kings exercise their power. And this is how wardrobes, liveries, chaperones, long hair, weathercocks, red heels, mitres, dovecots, church pillows and incense through the nose, nobiliary particles, ribbons, diadems, beauty marks, rouge, coronets, crackowes, mortiers, magistrate's cassocks, the Menu-vair, scarlet, spurs, etc., etc., have successively become the material signs of how much or how little rest a man is able to get, how many or how few whims he has the right to satisfy, how much or how little men, money, thoughts, and labor he is able to squander. In this way a passerby could distinguish, just by looking at him, a man of leisure from a worker, a numeral from a zero.

All of a sudden the Revolution, with one powerful hand, took this entire wardrobe that had evolved over fourteen centuries and reduced it to paper money, and thus madly brought about one of the greatest misfortunes to afflict a nation. Workers grew weary of working by themselves; they got it into their heads to share the sorrow and profit, in equal portions, with the miserable rich who didn't know how to do anything but enjoy themselves at their leisure! . . .

The entire world, bearing witness to this struggle, saw the very ones who were most enamored of this system outlaw it, declare it subversive, dangerous, impractical, and absurd, as soon as they were transformed from workers into men of leisure.

And so from this moment on, society reconstituted itself, rebaronized itself, recounticized itself, redecorated itself with ribbons, and the rooster's feathers took charge of teaching the poor what the heraldic pearls once said to them: *Vade retro, Satanas!* . . . Behind us, CIVVIES! . . . France, the eminently philosophical land that it is, having experienced through this last endeavor the usefulness, the sense of security of the old system through which nations had been built, returned, with the help of some soldiers, to the principle according to which the Trinity put valleys and mountains, oak trees and grasses into this lowly world.

And in the year of grace 1804, as in the year MCXX,[15] it was acknowledged that it was infinitely pleasant for a man or a woman to say to themselves when looking at their fellow citizens: "I am above them; I dazzle them, I protect them, I govern them, and every one of them can clearly see that I govern them, protect them, and dazzle them; for I am a man who dazzles, protects, or governs others, who speaks, eats, walks, drinks, sleeps, coughs, dresses, and enjoys himself differently than those dazzled, protected, and governed."

And ELEGANT LIVING suddenly appeared! . . .

And it soared, bright and new, utterly old, utterly young, proud, spruce, approved, corrected, augmented, and restored by this wonderfully moral, religious, monarchic, literary, constitutional, egoistic argument: "I dazzle, I protect, I . . . ," etc.

For the principles by which people with talent, power, or money conduct themselves and live shall never resemble those of the common herd.

And no one wants to be common! . . .

Elegant living is thus essentially the art of manners.

We now feel that the question has been sufficiently abridged and as subtly posed as if S.S. the Count Ravez himself had been in charge of proposing it to the first septennial Chamber.[16]

But with whom does elegant living begin, and are all men of leisure capable of following its principles?

Here are two aphorisms that should settle all doubts and serve as a starting point for our fashionable observations:

VII

Only the centaur, the man in Tilbury,[17] completely exemplifies elegant living.

VIII

It is not enough to become or to be born rich to lead an elegant life: one must feel it.

"Don't act the prince," said Solon before us, "if you haven't learned how to be one."[18]

Chapter II:
On the Feeling for Elegant Living

Only a complete understanding of social progress can produce the feeling for *elegant living*: does this way of living not express the new relations and needs created by a young, already virile social organization? In order to explain this feeling and see everyone adopt it, we must examine the series of causes that made elegant living appear within the very movement of our revolution—for it did not exist in the past.

Indeed, in times past the nobleman lived as he pleased and was always in a class of his own. But amidst this red-heeled people,[19] the ways of the courtier took over our investigations into the fashionable. Even then, the tone of the court only goes back to that of Catherine de Médicis. It was our two Italian queens[20] who imported the refinements of luxury, the grace of manners, and the enchantment of clothes into France. The work which Catherine began by introducing etiquette (see her letters to Charles IX), by surrounding the throne with intellectuals of superior quality, was continued by the Spanish queens,[21] a potent influence that rendered the court of France arbiter and depositary of the refinements invented, in succession, by the Moors and by Italy.

But until the reign of Louis XV, what distinguished the courtier from the nobleman could barely be discerned, and then only through the expense of their doublets, how flared their boots were, a ruff, how musky their hair was, or how new their words were. Such completely personal luxuries were never unified into a way of life. One hundred thousand ecus profusely thrown into clothing, into an equipage, were enough for an entire lifetime. In this way a provincial nobleman was able to dress badly and still know how to erect marvelous edifices, which today elicit our admiration and sow despair among the rich, whereas a sumptuously attired courtier would be greatly embarrassed to entertain two women at his home. A saltcellar by Benvenuto Cellini,[22] purchased for a king's ransom, was often set upon a table surrounded by benches.

In short, if we pass from material life to moral life, a nobleman could run up debts, live in taverns, not know how to write or speak, prostitute his character and talk nonsense, but he would still remain a nobleman. The executioner and the law still distinguished him from all specimens of the French peasant (an admirably classic example of busy people), by cutting off his head instead of hanging him. You would have thought him the *civis romanus* in France; for it was as if the Gauls,* treated as true slaves, did not exist.

This doctrine was so well understood that a woman of quality dressed in front of her servants as if they were oxen, and brought no dishonor upon herself by *pinching* the money of the middle class (see the conversation of the Duchess of Tallard in M. Barrière's latest work);[23] that the Countess of Egmont did not believe she had committed an infidelity by loving a villain; that Madame de Chaulnes maintained that a duchess was without age for a commoner; and that M. Joly de Fleury logically deemed the twenty million liable to the corvée as an accident in the State.[24]

Today the noblemen of 1804 or the year MCXX no longer represent anything. The Revolution was just a crusade against privileges, and its mission was not altogether in vain: for if the Chambre des pairs, the last scrap of hereditary prerogatives, becomes a territorial oligarchy, it shall never be an aristocracy armed with hostile rights. But despite the obvious improvement stamped upon the social order by the movement of 1789, the necessary social injustice constituted by the disparity in fortunes returned in a

* "Gentleman" meant: *man of the nation, gentis homo.*

new guise. Do we not have, in exchange for a ridiculous and fallen feudal system, the triple aristocracy of money, power, and talent, which, however lawful it may be, lays no less of an immense burden on the masses when it imposes on them the patriciate of the bank, the ministerialism and the ballastics of the papers and the tribune, all stepping stones for people of talent? And so while sanctioning, by its return to the constitutional monarchy, an illusory political equality, France has never done anything but generalize misfortune: for we are a democracy of the rich. Let us admit it, the great struggle of the eighteenth century was a remarkable fight between the third estate and the orders: the people were just the auxiliary of those most cunning. Consequently, only two types of men remain in October 1830: the rich and the poor, people in a carriage and people on foot, those who have paid for the right to be men of leisure and those who try to buy it. Society expresses itself in two terms, but the proposition remains the same. Men always owe the delights of life and power to chance, which long ago created noblemen; for talent is the luck of organization, the way patrimonial fortune is that of birth.

The man of leisure will thus always govern his fellow men: after examining things, after wearing them out, he feels the need to PLAY WITH MEN. Moreover, only he whose existence is secure is able to study, observe, and compare, only the rich man displays the invasive spirit inherent to the human soul in support of his intelligence: and so the triple power of time, money, and talent guarantees him the monopoly of the empire; for the man armed with thought took the place of the armor-clad banneret. Evil lost its strength by spreading itself out; intelligence became the mainspring of our civilization: such is all progress purchased through the blood of our fathers.

The aristocracy and the middle class are going to share, the former its traditions of elegance, good taste, and high policy, the latter its prodigious conquests in the arts and sciences; the two together shall then lead the people onto the path of civilization and light. But the princes of thought, power, or industry who form this enlarged caste shall still experience the same irresistible itching to make public, as did the noblemen of old, their degree of power, and even today social man exhausts his genius in finding distinctions. This feeling is probably a need of the soul, a kind of thirst; for even the savage has his feathers, his tattoos, his finely worked bows, his cowry shells, and fights over glass jewelry. So as the nineteenth century advances under the supervision of a thought whose goal is to substitute the exploitation of man by intelligence for the exploitation of man by man,* the continual promulgation of our

* This metaphysical expression of man's latest progress can help explain society's structure, and find the reasons for the phenomena offered by individual lives. Since busy living is never anything but *man's exploitation*

superiority will have to undergo the influence of this noble philosophy and partake much less of matter than of the soul.

Only yesterday the Franks, armorless, a weak and degenerate people, were continuing the rites of a dead religion and raising the banners of a faded strength. Now any man who is going to rise up will rely on his own strength. Men of leisure shall no longer be fetishes, but veritable gods. Thus the expression of our fortune will result in its employment, and the proof of our individual elevation will be found in our lives taken as a whole; for

---

of matter or *man's exploitation of man*, whereas the ARTIST'S LIFE and ELEGANT LIVING always presuppose *thought's exploitation of man*, it is easy, when applying these formulas to the degree of intelligence developed in human labor, to explain differences in fortune. Indeed, in politics and finances as in engineering, the result is always due to the strength of the means, QED (see page 12). Is this system bound to make us all millionaires some day? . . . We think not. Despite M. Jacotot's success, it is a mistake to think that minds are equal: they can only be so through a similarity in strength, exercise, or perfection that is impossible to find in the organs: because it would be difficult, especially among civilized men, to gather together two homogeneous organizations. This tremendous fact proves that Sterne was probably right to put the *art of having babies* before any science and philosophy. Some men will thus always remain poor, others rich: but as superior minds are on a path of progress, the well-being of the masses shall increase, as the history of civilization has demonstrated since the sixteenth century, that century when thought triumphed in Europe through the influence of Bacon, Descartes, and Bayle.

princes and peoples understand that the most energetic sign will no longer compensate for power. And so in the attempt to make a system through an image, there remain fewer than three representations of Napoléon in imperial clothes; instead we see him everywhere dressed in his little green uniform, wearing a three-cornered hat and crossing his arms. He is only poetic and true without the imperial charlatanism. By throwing him down from his column, his enemies only made him grow in stature. Stripped of royalty's showy rags, Napoléon becomes immense; he is the symbol of his century, an idea of the future. A powerful man is always unaffected and calm.

The moment that two books of parchment[25] no longer stand for everything, when the natural son of a millionaire bath attendant and a man of talent have the same rights as the son of a count, we can no longer be distinguished by anything but our intrinsic value. Differences have vanished in our society: all that remain are nuances. Consequently, good breeding, elegant manners, the *je ne sais quoi*, the fruits of a complete education—these form the only barrier separating the man of leisure from the busy man. If privilege exists, it stems from moral superiority. Hence the high price that the majority places on education, on the purity of language, on the grace of deportment, on the relatively easy manner in which an outfit is worn, on the careful choice of living quarters: in short, on the perfection of everything proceeding from the person. Do we not imprint our manners and thought on everything that surrounds us and belongs to us? "Speak, walk, eat, or dress yourself, and I will tell you what you are," has replaced the old proverb, the court expression, the adage of the privileged. A Marshal de Richelieu is impossible today. A peer of France, even a prince, risks falling beneath a one-hundred-ecu voter if he brings discredit upon himself, for no one is permitted to be impertinent or debauched. The more things are subjected to the influence of thought, the more life's details are ennobled, refined, and elevated.

Such is the imperceptible slope on which the Christianity of our revolution overthrew the polytheism of the feudal system, on what filiation a true feeling emanated into the very material and changing signs of our strength. And that is how we have returned to our starting point: the adoration of the golden calf. Except that the idol speaks, walks, thinks; in a word, it is a giant. And a packsaddle is thus placed on the poor French peasant for a long time. A popular revolution is impossible today. If some kings still fall, this will be, as it was in France, due to the cold contempt of the intelligent class.

To distinguish our life through elegance, it is no longer enough to be a nobleman or to draw the four winning numbers in some human lottery; one must still have been endowed with that indefinable faculty (perhaps the spirit of our senses!) that always prompts us to choose truly beautiful or good things, things whose unity matches our physiognomy and our fate. It is exquisite tact, the constant exercise of which alone can suddenly reveal relations, anticipate consequences, guess the place or significance of objects, words, ideas, and people; for—to sum up—the principle of elegant life is a noble thought of order and harmony, intended to give poetry to things. Hence this aphorism:

IX

A man becomes rich; he is born elegant.

Resting on such a foundation, seen from this height, this system of existence is no longer a fleeting joke, an empty word scorned by thinkers like an old newspaper. On the contrary: *elegant living* rests on the strictest deductions about the social construct. Is it not the very customs and manners of superior people, who know how to enjoy fortune and obtain the people's forgiveness for their loftiness in return for sharing the benefits of their insight? Is it not the expression of a country's progress, since it represents every kind of luxury? In short, if it is the sign of a perfected nature, shouldn't every man wish to study it and discover its secrets?

It is thus no longer a minor thing to scorn or adopt the short-lived dictates of FASHION, for *mens agitat molem*: a man's mind can be known by the manner in which he holds his walking stick. Distinctions depreciate or die when they become widespread; but there exists a power in charge of stipulating new ones, and that is opinion; and fashion has never been anything but opinion as regards dress. Dress being the most energetic of all symbols, the Revolution was also a question of fashion, a debate between silk and woolen cloth. But today, FASHION is no longer determined by a person's wealth. The material of life, once the object of general progress, has undergone tremendous developments. There is not a single one of our needs that has not produced an encyclopedia, and our animal life is tied to the universality of human knowledge. In dictating the laws of elegance, fashion encompasses all the arts. It is as much the principle of works of *art* as it is of works of *craft*.[26] Is it not the seal that unanimous consent places upon a discovery, or by which it marks the inventions that enrich man's well-being? Does it not constitute the always lucrative reward, the homage awarded to genius? By welcoming, by *indicating* progress, it takes the lead in everything: it brings about revolutions in music, literature, drawing, and architecture. A treatise on elegant living, being the combination of inalienable principles that must guide the expression of our thought through exterior life, is, as it were, the *metaphysics of things*.

Chapter III: Outline of This Treatise

"I just arrived from Pierrefonds, where I'd gone to see my uncle: he's rich, he has horses, only he doesn't know what a *tiger*,[27] a *groom*, or a *britschka* is, and he still goes about in a pump-spring cabriolet! . . ."

"So!" our honorable friend L.-M.[28] suddenly exclaimed . . . as he set his pipe down between the arms of a *Venus on a Turtle* that decorates his mantelpiece; "So! If it is a question of man as a whole, there is the code of the law of nations; the political code for a nation; the civil code for our interests; a code of procedure for our disagreements; a code of education for our freedom; the penal code for our aberrations; a commercial law for industry; a rural code for the country; a military code for soldiers; a black code for Negroes; a forestry code for our woods; a maritime law for our decked-out cockleshells . . .

In short, we have codified everything, from the funeral procession of the court, to the quantity of tears we must shed for a king, an uncle, a cousin, and that includes life and even the gait of a service horse . . ."

"Well, what of it?" E. de G. . . . said to him, not noticing that our honorable friend was getting his breath back.

"Well," he replied, "when these codes were made, some sort of epizooty (he meant to say epidemic) took hold of the cacographers, and they inundated us with codes . . . Good manners, gourmandism, the theater, decent people, women, indemnity, colonists, and administration—everything had its code. Then Saint-Simon's doctrine towered over this ocean of works, claiming that *codification* (see *L'Organisateur*[29]) was a special science . . . Perhaps the typographer made a mistake and misread *caudification*, from *cauda*, tail . . . but it doesn't matter . . .

"I ask you," he added, stopping one of his listeners and drawing him in by a button, "is it not a true miracle that *elegant living* has not found legislators among all these writing and thinking people? Those handbooks, even the ones for rural policemen, the mayor, and the taxpayer: are they not trifles compared to a treatise on FASHION? Would not the publication of the principles that make life poetic be of tremendous use? If in the provinces the majority of our farms, vineyards, smallholdings, houses, metairies, sharecroppings, etc., are veritable kennels; if the livestock, and particularly the horses, are treated in France in a manner unworthy of a Christian people; if the science of comfort, if the immortal Fumade's lighter, if Lemare's coffee maker, if cheap carpets are unknown sixty leagues outside of Paris, it is quite certain that this general lack of the most mundane inventions owed to modern science comes from the ignorance in which we let country gentlemen wallow! Elegance attaches itself to everything. It tends to make a nation less poor by inspiring in it a taste for luxury, for if there was ever a great axiom, it is certainly this:

X

The fortune one acquires is in proportion
to the needs one creates.

"It (still elegance) gives a more picturesque look to a country, and improves agriculture; for the beauty of an animal's race and produce depends on the care given to its living and shelter. Go take a look at the holes in which the Bretons lodge their cows, their horses, their sheep, and their children, and you will have to admit that of all the books to be made, a treatise on elegance would be the most philanthropic and patriotic. If a secretary left his handkerchief and snuffbox on the table of Louis XVIII, if the mirrors in an old countryman's home provide the young elegant man shaving the appearance of someone about to fall into apoplexy, and if, finally, your uncle still goes about in a pump-spring cabriolet, it is assuredly for want of a classic work on FASHION! . . ."

Our honorable friend spoke for a long while, and very well, with that ease of elocution which those envious call *prattling*; then he concluded by saying: "Elegance dramatizes life . . ."

Oh, that word roused a general cheer! The sagacious E. de G . . . showed that the drama could hardly result from the uniformity stamped by elegance onto a country's customs, and comparing England to Spain, he proved his thesis by enriching his argumentation with the local colors which the customs of those two countries provided him. Then he finished in this manner:

"It is easy, messieurs, to explain this deficiency in science. What young or old man would be bold enough to take on such an overwhelming responsibility? To undertake a treatise on elegant living, one would have to have unbelievably fanatical self-esteem; for it would be an attempt to surpass the elegant people of Paris, and they themselves proceed by trial and error, trying and not always managing to attain grace."

At this moment, ample libations having been made in honor of the fashionable goddess of tea, everyone's spirits had risen to the pitch of illuminism. Then one of the most elegant* sub-editors for *La Mode* stood up and cast a triumphant look upon his colleagues:

* Here, the elegance applies to the clothes.

"This man exists," he said.

General laughter greeted this exordium, but silent admiration soon followed when he added:

"BRUMMELL! . . . Brummell is in Boulogne, banished from England by too many creditors who were quick to forget the services which this patriarch of fashion rendered unto his country! . . ."

And suddenly the publication of a treatise on elegant living seemed easy and it was unanimously decided on *as being a great benefit* to humanity, and an enormous step along the path of progress.

Needless to say, we owe to Brummell the philosophical inductions by which we were able to demonstrate in the two preceding chapters how elegant living is closely bound to the perfection of every human society; the former friends of this immortal creator of English luxury will have, we hope, recognized the lofty philosophy through the imperfect translation of his thoughts.

It would be difficult to express the feeling that took hold of us when we saw this prince of fashion: it was one of both respect and joy. How not purse one's lips enigmatically when seeing the man who had invented the philosophy of furniture and vests, and who was going to pass on to us axioms on pants, grace, and harnesses?

But how not also be filled with admiration for George IV's closest friend, for the *fashionable* who had laid down laws on England, and given to the Prince of Wales that taste for clothing and *comfortabilism* that was worth such promotion to well-dressed officers?* Was he not living proof of the influence exercised by fashion? But when we thought that Brummell's life was, at that moment, full of bitterness, and that Boulogne was his Saint Helena, all our feelings merged in respectful enthusiasm.

We saw him just as he was getting up. His dressing gown bore the mark of his misfortune; but although conforming to that, it harmonized admirably with the accessories of his apartment. Brummell, old and poor, was still Brummell: only a portliness equal to that of George IV had broken the happy frame of that model body, and the ex-God of dandyism was wearing a wig! . . . Dreadful lesson! . . . Brummell, thus! . . . Was this not Sheridan dead drunk when Parliament ended, or seized by the bailiff's assistant?[30]

Brummell in a wig; Napoleon in a garden; Kant in infancy; Louis XVI in a red bonnet; and Charles X in Cherbourg! . . . Such are the five greatest spectacles of our era.

The great man welcomed us in a perfect tone of voice. His modesty was all it took to captivate us. He seemed flattered by the apostolate we had reserved for

---

* When George IV saw a serviceman dressed with care, he rarely failed to honor and promote him. On the same token, he greeted people without elegance very badly.

him; but as he thanked us, he declared that he did not believe himself talented enough to accomplish such a delicate mission.

"Luckily," he told us, "I have in Boulogne several first-rate gentlemen for companions, who have been led to France by the overly generous manner in which they conceived of elegant living in London . . . *Honneur au courage malheureux!*" he added, taking off his hat and flashing us a glance as merry as it was derisive. "So," he resumed, "we will be able to form an illustrious and experienced enough committee here as a last resort for deciding on this life's most serious difficulties, so seemingly frivolous on the face of it, and when *vos amis de Paris* accept or reject our maxims, let us hope that your undertaking will present a monumental character!"

This said, he suggested we have a cup of tea with him. We accepted. A mistress, still elegant despite her portliness, had come out of the adjoining room to do the honors of the teapot, and we noticed that Brummell had his Marchioness Conyngham as well.[31] So the number of *crowns* alone was able to distinguish him from his royal friend George IV. Alas! They are now *ambo pares*,[32] both dead, or just about.

Our first meeting took place during this lunch, the studied elegance of which proved to us that Brummell's ruin would be Paris's fortune.

The question occupying us was a question of life or death to our undertaking.

Indeed, if the feeling for elegant living had to result from a relatively fortuitous arrangement, it followed that for us, men were divided into two classes: poets and prose-writers, elegant men and the common run of martyrs; consequently, no more treatise: the former knew everything already, and the latter were unable to learn anything.

But after a most memorable discussion, we saw this consolatory axiom take form:

XI

Though elegance is less an art than a feeling, it is also the result of instinct and habit.

"Yes!" exclaimed William Crad . . . k, Brummell's loyal companion,[33] "reassure the timid population of country gentlemen, shopkeepers, and bankers . . . Not all the aristocracy's children are born with a feeling for elegance, with that taste that helps give life its poetic stamp; and yet every country's aristocracy distinguishes itself by its manners and by a remarkable understanding of life!—What is this privilege, then?—Education, habit. From the time they are in the cradle, struck with the harmonious grace reigning about them, raised by elegant mothers whose language and manners retain all the good traditions, the children of fine gentlemen familiarize themselves with the rudiments of our science, and it takes a surly nature to resist the constant appearance of truly beautiful things.

So the most hideous spectacle for a nation is the fall of a great man beneath the level of a mere bourgeois.

"If intellects are not all equal, it is rare that our senses are not: for the intellect results from inner perfection; the more we broaden the form, the more we achieve equality: and so human legs resemble each other much better than faces do, thanks to the shape of those limbs, which present lengthened lines. Now elegance, being simply the perfection of perceptible objects, must be accessible to everyone out of habit. Study can lead a rich man to wear boots and pants just as well as we do, and teach him how to spend his fortune with grace . . . And the same goes for everything else."

Brummell gave a slight frown. We could see that he was about to utilize that prophetic voice, the dictates of which a nation's wealthy people had followed not long ago.

"The axiom is true," he said, "and I approve of part of the honorable speaker's reasoning; but I strongly protest removing in this manner the barrier separating elegant living from everyday life and opening the temple doors to an entire people. No!" exclaimed Brummell, striking his fist on the table, "no, all legs are not called upon to wear a boot or a pair of pants in the same way . . . No, Milords. Will there not always be those that limp, those deformed or ignoble? And is that sentence we utter a thousand times in the course of our lives not an axiom?

XII

Nothing resembles a man less than a man!

"Therefore," he resumed, "after establishing the favorable principle which leaves to novices of elegant living the hope of attaining grace through habit, let us also recognize the exceptions, and in good faith seek formulas for them."

After many efforts, after numerous observations learnedly debated, we wrote out the following axioms:

XIII

One must have studied at least as far as rhetoric to lead an elegant life.

XIV

Retailers, businessmen, and teachers of the humanities fall outside the scope of elegant living.

XV

The miser is a negation.

XVI

A banker who reaches the age of forty without having gone into voluntary liquidation, or who has more than thirty-six inches in girth, is the damned soul of elegant living: he will see paradise without ever entering it.

XVII

Anyone who does not frequently visit Paris will never be completely elegant.

XVIII

*The impolite man is the leper of the fashionable world.**

"Enough!" said Brummell. "If we add any more aphorisms, they will be included in the teaching of general principles, which should comprise the subject of the second part of the treatise."

Then he deigned to set down the limits of the science by dividing up our work in this manner:

"If you examine carefully," he said, "all the material translations of thought in which elegant living consists, you will no doubt be struck, as I was, by the relatively intimate parallel that exists between certain things and our person. Speech, gait, manners: these are acts that proceed *directly* from a man, and which are wholly subject to the laws of elegance. The table, people, horses, carriages, furniture, the upkeep of houses: these only stem, so to

---

* The knowledge of the most commonplace laws of courtesy being one of the components of our science, we take this opportunity to pay public tribute to Father Gaultier,[34] whose work on courtesy must be looked upon as being the most complete work on the subject, and as an admirable treatise on moral doctrine.

speak, *indirectly* from the individual. Although these accessories of existence also bear the character of elegance, which we stamp on everything that proceeds from us, they seem, as it were, removed from the seat of thought, and should only hold second place in this far-reaching theory of elegance. Is it not natural to mirror the great thought that drives our century in a work perhaps intended to react against the manners of Ignorantines of fashion? Let us here acknowledge, then, that all principles directly relating to intelligence will have top place in this aristocratic encyclopedia. However, messieurs," Brummell added, "there is one fact that towers over all others. Man dresses himself before acting, before speaking, before walking, and before eating; the actions belonging to fashion, deportment, conversation, etc., are always just the consequences of our clothes. That admirable observer, Sterne, declared, in the wittiest manner, that the ideas of the shaven man are not those of the bearded.[35] We are all under the influence of clothing. The dressed artist stops working. A woman changes quite a bit between wearing a dressing gown or being decked out for the ball: you could say that they are two different women altogether!"

Here Brummell sighed.

"Our morning manners are no longer those of the evening," he resumed. "After all, George IV, whose friendship did me such honor, certainly thought he was greater the day of his coronation than on the day after. Clothes are the most tremendous modification social man has experienced; they influence all of existence. I do not think I am going against logic when I propose that you organize your work in this manner: After dictating the general laws of elegant living in your second part," he resumed, "you should devote the third to those things proceeding directly from the individual, with clothing at the beginning. Then, in my opinion, the fourth part would be set aside for those things that proceed directly from the person, which I regard as ACCESSORIES."

We forgive Brummell's predilection for clothes: they made his glory. It is perhaps a great man's folly, but we dared not oppose it and risk seeing this well-formulated classification get rejected by elegantologists of all countries. We decided to go along with Brummell's error.

And so the subject matter to be dealt with in the second part was adopted unanimously by this illustrious parliament of fashionophiles, under the title: GENERAL PRINCIPLES of elegant living.

The third part, concerning THINGS PROCEEDING DIRECTLY FROM THE PERSON, would be divided into several chapters.

The first will comprise *clothing in all its parts.* An initial paragraph will be devoted to *men's clothing*, a second to *women's clothing*; a third will offer an *essay* on *perfumes*, *baths*, and *hairdressing.*

Another chapter will provide a *complete theory on walking and deportment.*[36]

One of my best friends, M. Eugène Sue,[37] as remarkable for the elegance of his style and the originality of his insights as for his exquisite taste in things and his marvelous understanding of life, promised us his comments for a chapter entitled: *On impertinence considered in its relations to morals, religion, politics, the arts, and literature.*

The discussion got heated on the last two divisions. The question was whether the chapter on *Manners* had to come before the one on *Conversation.*

Brummell put an end to the discussion with an improvisation, which we are regretfully unable to convey in its entirety. He finished in this manner:

"Messieurs, were we in England, actions would necessarily come before words, for my compatriots are generally taciturn; but I have had the opportunity to observe that in France you always talk a lot before acting."

The fourth part, devoted to ACCESSORIES, will consist of the principles that must govern apartments, furniture, the table, horses, people, and carriages, and we will end with a treatise on the *art of receiving, be it in the city or in the country*, and on the *art of conducting oneself at the homes of others.*

In this manner we will have encompassed the universality of the most far-reaching of all sciences: that which occupies every moment of our life, which governs every act of our waking hours and the instruments of our sleep; for it still prevails throughout the silence of the nights.

Second Part: General Principles

MONOGRAPH ON VIRTUE

Consider also, madame, that there are
revolting perfections.
(*Unpublished work by the author*)

Chapter IV: Dogmas

The Church recognizes seven deadly sins and acknowledges only three theological virtues. We therefore have seven principles of remorse for three sources of consolation! It is a sad problem: 3 : 7 : : man : x . . . Not a single human creature, and we exclude neither Saint Teresa nor Saint Francis of Assisi, has been able to escape the consequences of this fatal proposition.

Despite its rigor, this dogma governs the elegant world the same way it conducts the Catholic world. Evil is relative, but good follows a severe line. From this eternal law, we can extract an axiom confirmed by every dictionary on *matters of conscience*:

XIX

Good has but one style; evil a thousand.

And so elegant living has its deadly sins and its three cardinal virtues. Yes, elegance is one, indivisible, like the Trinity, like liberty, like virtue. From this follows the most important of all our general aphorisms:

XX

The constituent principle of elegance is unity.

XXI

Unity is impossible without cleanliness, harmony, and relative simplicity.

But it is not simplicity rather than harmony, or harmony rather than cleanliness that produces elegance: elegance is born from a mysterious concordance between these three primordial virtues. To create it suddenly everywhere is the secret of innately distinguished spirits.

When analyzing any instances of bad taste that taint a stranger's clothing, apartments, speech, or deportment, observers will always find that they sin through relatively perceptible violations of this triple law of unity.

The exterior life is a sort of organized system that represents a man as accurately as a snail's colors recur on its shell. In the elegant life, everything is linked and connected. When M. Cuvier[38] sees the frontal bone, jawbone, or femoral bone of some beast, does he not infer an entire creature from them, even if it be antediluvian, and does he not immediately reconstruct a classified individual, be it saurian or marsupial, carnivorous or herbivorous? . . . This man never erred: his genius unveiled the unitary laws of animal life.

It is the same with the elegant life: a single chair determines an entire series of furnishings, the way a spur allows one to presuppose a horse. Certain clothing announces a certain sphere of nobility and good taste. Every fortune has its base and its summit. The Georges Cuviers of elegance never run the risk of passing erroneous judgment: they will tell you how many zeros, in the amount of revenues, should go with painting galleries, thoroughbred horses, Savonnerie carpets, diaphanous silk curtains, mosaic mantelpieces, Etruscan vases, and clocks surmounted by a statue escaped from the chisel of a David or Cortot.[39] Bring them a single coat peg: they will deduce an entire boudoir, a bedroom, a palace.

Unity rigorously demands this whole, which makes every accessory of existence interdependent; for a man of taste judges, like an artist, based on a mere nothing. The more perfect the whole is, the more noticeable will be a barbarism in it. Only a fool or a man of genius could put a candle into a cat-o'-nine-tails. The applications of this great fashionable law were well understood by the famous woman (Madame T . . .)[40] to whom we owe this aphorism:

XXII

One knows the mind of a hostess just
by stepping over her doorstep.

This far-reaching and perpetual image that represents* your fortune must never be an unfaithful specimen, for that would place you between two pitfalls: avarice or impotence. If you were too vain or too modest, you would no longer follow the dictates of this unity, whose least consequence would bring about a happy balance between your productive forces and your exterior form.

Such a cardinal error entails an entire physiognomy.

As the first term of this proposition, avarice has already been judged; but, without actually being guilty of such a disgraceful vice, many people, intent on obtaining a twofold result, try to lead an elegant life economically. They certainly achieve one objective: they are ridiculous. Do they not constantly resemble clumsy stagehands whose decorations offer a glimpse of the springs, counterweights, and the wings? For this reason they lack understanding of these two fundamental axioms of the science:

XXIII

The most essential effect in elegance is the concealment of one's means.

XXIV

Anything that reveals thrift is inelegant.

* These words *represent*, *representation*, have no other origin.

Indeed, thrift is a means. It is the nerve of good management, but it is like the oil that makes a machine's wheels run fluidly and smoothly: one should not see it or sense it.

These drawbacks are not the only castigations that parsimonious people bring upon themselves. By curbing the development of their existence, they step down from their sphere, and despite their power, they put themselves at the level of those whom vanity pushes toward the opposing pitfall. Who would not shudder at this dreadful brotherhood?

How many times have you encountered, in the city or in the country, semiaristocratic members of the middle class who, adorned to excess, are obliged, for lack of equipage, to plan their visits, their pleasures, and their duties according to the pronouncements of Matthieu Laensberg?[41] A slave to her hat, madame dreads the rain, and monsieur fears the sun or the dust. As impressible as barometers, they foretell the weather, drop everything and vanish at the sight of a cloud. Wet and covered in mud, they blame each other, back at their abode, for their woes; uncomfortable everywhere, they enjoy nothing.

This doctrine was summed up by an aphorism applicable to every existence, from that of the woman forced to hitch up her dress to sit down in a carriage, to the little German prince who is in need of a meal:

XXV

Harmony between exterior life and fortune results in ease.

The religious observation of this principle alone allows a man to deploy, even in his smallest actions, a liberty without which grace could not exist. If he measures his desires by his strength, he remains in his sphere without the fear of demeaning himself. This safety in action, which one could call the *consciousness of comfort*, protects us from the turmoil a poorly understood vanity can bring on.

Experts on elegant living do not lay out long paths of green cloth on their rugs, and for them the visits of an elderly asthmatic uncle are not to be dreaded. They do not consult the thermometer before going out with their horses. As subject to the burdens of fortune as they are to its benefits, they never seem bothered by a setback; for with them, everything is mended with money or resolved by the degree of their servants' effort. To put a vase or a clock in a casing, to protect their divans with dust covers, to pack up a chandelier: is all this not like those good people who, after having saved up their piggybanks to buy candelabra, immediately cover them with thick gauze? The man of taste must enjoy everything he owns. Like Fontenelle, *he doesn't like things that demand too much respect.*[42] Like nature, he is not afraid of flaunting his splendor on a daily basis: he can reproduce it. He also does not wait until, like the veterans of Luxembourg, his furniture pieces testify their services through numerous military chevrons to change their place, and he never complains about the excessive price of things because he has anticipated everything. For the man of the *busy life*, receptions are formal occasions; he has his periodical *consecrations* for which he does his unpacking, empties his wardrobes, and uncovers his bronzes; but the man of the *elegant life* knows to receive at any hour without letting himself be surprised. His motto is that of a family whose glory is joined with the discovery of a new world; new, he is *semper paratus*, always ready, always remaining himself. His house, his servants, his carriages, and his wealth are all unaware of the prejudice of Sunday. Every day is a holiday. Lastly, *si magna licet componere parvis*, he is like the famous Dessein[43] who replied, without coming out, when he learned of the arrival of the Duke of York:

"Put him in number four."

Or like the Duchesse d'Abrantès[44] who, beseeched by Napoléon to receive the Princess of Westphalie at Raincy, offered the very next day the pleasures of a royal hunt, opulent feasts, and a lavish ball to the sovereigns.

Every fashionable must imitate, in his sphere, this broad understanding of existence: he will easily achieve these wonderful results through constant research, through an exquisite freshness in details. Care and attention perpetuates the good grace of the whole, and from that comes this English axiom:

XXVI

Upkeep is the sine qua non *of elegance.*

Upkeep is not only this vital condition of cleanliness that obliges us to stamp things with their daily luster: the word expresses an entire system.

The moment that the finesse and grace of fabric replaced, in the European costume, the heaviness of golden woolen cloths and emblazoned coats of the laborious Middle Ages, a huge revolution had taken place in the things that make up life. Instead of burying a sum of money in perishable furniture, we used its interest for objects that were lighter, less expensive, and easier to replace, and families were no longer disinherited of capital.*

This calculation of an advanced civilization received its final developments in England. In that homeland of the comfortable, the material of life is looked upon as a great garment that is essentially mutable and subject to the whims of fashion. The rich annually change their horses, their carriages, their furniture; even diamonds are reset; everything takes on a new form. The slightest piece of furniture is also manufactured in this spirit; raw materials are wisely economized. If we have not yet

---

* Bassompierre's[45] clothes, which we cite because of the vulgarity of the fact, cost a hundred thousand ecus of our current money. Today the most elegant man spends no more than fifteen thousand francs on his clothes and replaces his clothing every season. The difference in capital used constitutes the differences in wealth, which does not destroy this observation: it applies to women's clothes and every part of our science.

attained this degree of science, we have nonetheless made some progress. The inelegant carpentry of the Empire is fully condemned, as are its heavy carriages and sculptures, semi-masterpieces that satisfy neither the artist nor the man of taste. We are finally making our way toward elegance and simplicity. If the modesty of our fortunes does not yet allow for such frequent transformations, we have at least understood this aphorism, which towers over current customs:

XXVII

Luxury is less expensive than elegance.

And we are starting to move away from the system by which our ancestors considered the acquisition of a piece of furniture to be an investment of a sum of money; for everyone instinctively sensed that it was both more elegant and more comfortable to eat on a set of plain china than to show to anyone interested a dish on which Constantin had copied the *Fornarina*.[46] The arts give birth to marvels that people must leave to kings, and monuments that belong only to nations. The man silly enough to introduce into the whole of his life a single example of a superior existence is trying to appear as something he is not, and thus slips back into that helplessness whose absurdities we have endeavored to condemn. We have therefore written the following maxim to enlighten victims of this mania for greatness:

XXVIII

As elegant living is a skillful development of self-respect, anything that displays too much vanity brings about a pleonasm.

Quite admirable! . . . Every general principle of science is but the corollary of the great principle we have proclaimed; for upkeep and its laws are, as it were, the immediate consequence of *unity*.

A good many people have objected to the enormity of the expenditure called for by our despotic aphorisms . . .

"What fortune," they tell us, "could meet the demands of your theories? . . . The day after a house has been refurnished, recarpeted, after a carriage has been restored, after the silk of a boudoir has been changed, does a *fashionable* not come to brazenly lean his pomaded head against a drape? Does an angry man not come specially to dirty a carpet? Do oafs not bump into the carriage? And can one always prevent impertinent people from crossing the sacred doorway of the boudoir?"

These objections, raised with that specious art with which women know how to color all their defenses, have been pulled to pieces by this aphorism:

XXIX

A man of good company no longer believes himself master of all the things that, in his home, must be put at the disposal of others.

An elegant man does not exactly say, as the king does, *our* carriage, *our* palace, *our* castle, or *our* horses; but he knows how to imprint every one of his actions with this royal refinement—a happy metamorphosis by which a man seems to invite to share in his fortune all those with whom he surrounds himself. Therefore this noble doctrine implies another axiom, no less important than the preceding one:

XXX

To receive a person into your home is to assume that he is worthy of dwelling in your sphere.

So the alleged mishaps for which a little housewife would demand satisfaction from our absolute dogmas could only come from an unpardonable lack of tact. Can a hostess ever complain of a lack of consideration or attention? Is it not her own fault? Are there not, for decent well-bred people, Masonic signs by which they are to recognize each other? By receiving only his equals into his private life, the elegant man has no more accidents to fear; should any occur, they would be blows dealt by fate that no one can avoid. The antechamber is an institution in England, where the aristocracy has made such great progress: houses without a parlor are rare. This room is intended for giving audience to any inferiors. The relative distance separating our men of leisure from busy men is represented by etiquette. Philosophers, Frondeurs, those who laugh, who make fun of ceremony, would not receive their grocer, be he representative of a large electoral body, with the same attention they bestow upon a marquis. It does not follow that fashionables despise workers: far from it, they have for them an admirable phrase of social respect: "They are *respectable people.*"

It is as tactless for an elegant man to make fun of the industrial class as it is to torment honeybees, as it is to disturb an artist working: it is in bad taste.

Salons belong, then, to those who have an *elegant thumb*, the way gardens belong to those who have a *green thumb.* If you have accepted our prolegomena, you have to accept all its consequences.

From this doctrine stems a fundamental aphorism:

XXXI

Superiority no longer exists in elegant living: there one treats power with power.

A man of good company never says: "I have the honor, etc." He is the humble servant of no man.

The sense of propriety today dictates new expressions, which people of taste adapt to circumstances. In this respect, we advise sterile minds to consult the *Letters of Montesquieu.* That renowned writer displayed a rare flexibility in talent in the manner with which he concluded even the slightest note, loathing as he did the absurd monograph of "I have the honor of being..."

Since people of elegant living represent the natural aristocracies of a country, they owe each other the same consideration of utter equality. As talent, money, and power provide equal entitlements for all, the man who is seemingly weak and in need, and to whom you tactlessly direct a slight nod of the head, shall soon be at the summit of the State, and he whom you greet obsequiously shall tomorrow return to the nothingness of fortune without influence.

Up to now, all our dogmas have embraced more the spirit than the form of things. We have presented, as it were, the *aesthetics* of elegant living. In our attempt to determine the general laws that govern the details, we have been less amazed than surprised to discover a sort of similarity between architectural principles and those we have yet to spell out. So we asked ourselves whether, by any chance, the majority of the objects useful to elegant living were not to be found in the field of architecture. The article of clothing, the bed, the coupé are all shelters for the person, the way a house is the great article of clothing that covers man and the things he uses. It seems that we have employed everything, even language, as M. de Talleyrand[47] said, to disguise a life, a thought, that nevertheless, despite our efforts, pierces through every veil.

Without wishing to grant this idea more importance than it merits, we will record here some of the rules that follow from it:

XXXII

Elegance imperiously demands that means be in accordance with the goal.

From this principle stem two other aphorisms that are its direct consequence.

XXXIII

The man of taste must always know how to reduce need to a minimum.

XXXIV

Each thing must appear as it is.

XXXV

A profusion of ornament works against its intended effect.

XXXVI

Ornament must be set up high.

XXXVII

A multiplicity of colors will always be in bad taste.

We will not attempt to demonstrate the soundness of these axioms here through some applications, because we shall elaborate upon their consequences more rationally in the following two parts, and indicate their effects on every detail. This observation leads us to omit from this part the general principles that prevail over each of the subsidiary divisions of the science, feeling that they would be better placed in the form of summaries at the beginning of those chapters whose subject matter they govern more directly.

Moreover, all the precepts we have already proclaimed, and to which we shall subsequently often be compelled to make recourse, shall seem commonplace to many people.

We would accept this reproach as praise. Nevertheless, despite the simplicity of these laws, which more than one elegantologist would have perhaps been able to write, deduce, or link together in a better fashion, we will not come to a close without pointing out to neophytes of fashion that good taste results not so much from the knowledge of these rules as from their application. A man must practice this science with the same ease with which he speaks his mother tongue. It is dangerous to stammer in the elegant world. Have you not often seen those semi-fashionables who wear themselves out by running after grace, who are embarrassed if they see the slightest crease in their shirt, and sweat blood to attain a false propriety, like those poor Englishmen who take out their *pocket*[48] at every word? Do you recall, poor cretins of elegant living, that our XXXIIIrd aphorism essentially produces this other principle, your eternal condemnation:

XXXVIII

Studied elegance is to true elegance what a wig is to hair.

This maxim implies the following, and accordingly harsh, corollary:

XXXIX

Dandyism *is a heresy of elegant life.*

In effect, dandyism is an affectation of fashion. In playing the dandy, a man becomes a piece of furniture for the boudoir, an extremely ingenious mannequin that can sit upon a horse or a couch, that bites or sucks on the end of a walking stick by habit—but a thinking being . . . never! The man who sees only fashion in fashion is a fool. Elegant living excludes neither thought nor science: it sanctions them. It must learn not only how to enjoy time, but to employ it in accordance with an extremely high order of ideas.

Since when we started this second part of our treatise, we found some similarity between our dogmas and those of Christianity, we will close by borrowing from theology some scholastic terms suitable for expressing the results obtained by those who know how to apply our principles with relative skill.

A new man appears, his attire is in good taste; he receives guests marvelously well, his servants are not coarse; he gives excellent dinner parties; he is well up on fashion, politics, new sayings, and ephemeral customs; he even creates them; in short, everything at his home is characterized by a rigorous comfortabilism. He is, as it were, the *Methodist* of elegance, and walks in a manner worthy of the century. Neither perfectly graceful nor unpleasant, you will never hear an indecorous word from him, and he never betrays himself by an unseemly gesture . . . We need not finish this portrayal; this man has *sufficient grace.*

Do we not all know an amiable egoist who possesses the secret of telling us about himself without overly displeasing us? With him, everything is graceful, fresh, meticulous, even poetic. He makes himself envied. As you share in his interests and pleasures, in his wealth, he seems to feel concern about your lack of fortune. His obligingness, in all his speech, is a sophisticated courtesy. For him, friendship is but a theme whose richness he knows admirably well, and whose modulations he assesses in tune with every person.

His life is imprinted with perpetual personality, by which he obtains forgiveness because of his manners: artistic with artists, old with an old man, a child with children, he captivates without pleasing, for he tells us lies out of self-interest and amuses us through ulterior motives. He looks after us and is affectionate with us because he is bored, and if today we notice that we have been played, tomorrow we shall again go back to be deceived . . . This man has *essential grace.*

But there is a person whose harmonious voice marks his speech with a charm that is equally widespread in his manners. He knows when to speak and when to stay silent, takes a tactful interest in you, employs only appropriate subjects for conversation; his words are well chosen; his language is pure, his mockery flatters, and his criticism does not offend. Far from being at variance from you with the ignorant self-assurance of a fool, he seems to seek in your company good sense or truth. He does not hold forth any more than he fights; he takes pleasure in leading a discussion that he brings to an end at the right moment. Even-tempered, his manner is affable and pleasant. There is nothing forced about his courtesy, his attentiveness is not the slightest bit servile; he reduces respect to nothing more than a gentle shadow; he never tires you, and leaves you feeling pleased with him and with yourself. Led into his sphere through an inexplicable magneticism, you will recall his spirit of good grace imprinted on the things that surround him; everything about him delights the eye and allows you to breathe as if it were the air of your homeland. In private life, this person charms you with an innocent tone. He is unaffected. Never any effort, any excessive display of wealth, any flaunting; his feelings are rendered simply because they are real. He is frank, and never offends another's pride. He accepts men as God does, forgiving faults and silly ways, understanding every age and never feeling any irritation, because he is tactful enough to anticipate anything. He obliges you to him before consoling, he is loving and cheerful: and so you will love him irresistibly. You take him for a classic example and devote a cult to him.

This person has *divine and concomitant grace.*

Charles Nodier knew how to personify this ideal being in his *Oudet,* a graceful figure unharmed by the magic of the brush.[49] But it is nothing to read his leaflet: one must hear Nodier himself recounting certain particularities that stem too much from private life to be written, and then you will understand the prestigious allure of these privileged creatures . . .

This magnetic power is the great aim of elegant life. We must try everything to lay hold of it; but a successful outcome is always difficult, for the cause of success lies within a beautiful soul. Happy are those who exercise it! It is so nice to see everything appeal to us, and to nature and to men! . . .

Now that we have covered the grand outlines, we shall deal with the details.

Third Part: On Things That Come Directly from the Person

"Do you think that one can be a man of talent without all of this nonsense?"
"Yes, monsieur, but you will be a more or less amiable, well- or bad-mannered man of talent," she replied.

Strangers chatting in a salon

Chapter V: On Clothing in All Its Parts

We owe M. Auger,[50] a young writer whose philosophical spirit has provided gravity to the most frivolous questions of fashion, a thought that we will turn into an axiom:

XL

Clothing is how society expresses itself.

This maxim sums up all our doctrines and virtually contains them to such a degree that anything more that can be said is just a further development of this learned aphorism.

The scholar or the elegant socialite who would like to determine the costumes of a people in each age would in this manner assemble the most picturesque and most nationally true history. To explain the long hair of the Franks, the tonsure of the monks, the shaven head of the serf, the wigs of Popocambou, the aristocratic powder and the titus cuts of 1790:[51] would this not recount our country's principal revolutions? To ask the origin of crackowes, purses, hoods, panniers, farthingales, gloves, masks, and velvet is to entail a *fashionologue* in the appalling maze of sumptuary laws and on every battlefield on which civilization triumphed over the unrefined customs that the barbarism of the Middle Ages introduced to Europe. If the Church successively excommunicated the priests who put on breeches and those who gave them up for pants, if the wig of the canons of Beauvais once took over the Parliament of Paris for half a century, it is because these seemingly trivial things represented either ideas or interests: whether it be the foot, the bust, or the head, you will always see social progress, a reactionary system, or some fierce struggle expressed through the aid of some article of clothing. Sometimes a shoe announces a privilege; sometimes a hood, bonnet, or hat signals a revolution; here, a piece of embroidery, or a scarf; there, ribbons or some straw adornment expresses a party: and so you belong to the Crusaders, to the Protestants, to the Guises, to the League, to the Béarn, or to the Fronde.

Do you have a green bonnet? You are a man without honor.

Do you have a yellow wheel by way of decoration on your surcot? Move on, outcast of Christianity! . . . Jew, go back to your hole at curfew or be punished by a fine.

Ah, young girl! You have gold rings, wonderful necklaces, and pendant earrings that blaze like your fiery eyes! . . . Watch out! If the policeman sees you, he will take you into custody and you will be imprisoned for having hurried through the town like that, mad about your body, running through the streets where you make the eyes of old men flash as you bankrupt them! . . .

Do you have white hands? . . . Your throat is cut to the cries of "Long live Jacques Bonhomme! Death to the lords!"

Do you have a Saint Andrew's cross? . . . Enter Paris without fear: John the Fearless reigns there.

Do you wear the revolutionary cockade? . . . Flee! . . . Marseilles would murder you, for the final cannons of Waterloo spit out death and old Bourbons at us!

So why would clothing always be the most eloquent of styles if it were not really the whole man, man with his political opinions, man with the text of his existence, man made into a hieroglyph? Even today, *clothingonomy* has become almost a branch of the art created by Gall and Lavater.[32] Although we now nearly all dress in the same manner, it is easy for an observer to pick out in a crowd, in an assembly, at the theater, or on a stroll, the man of the Marais, of the faubourg Saint-Germain, of the Latin quarter, or of the Chaussée-d'Antin; the proletariat, the proprietor, the consumer and the producer, the lawyer and the serviceman, the man who talks and the man who acts.

The quartermasters of our armies do not recognize the uniforms of our regiments any more promptly than the physiologist distinguishes the liveries imposed on man by wealth, work, or misery.

Draw up a hat stand there, put on some clothes! . . . Good! If you do not want to walk about like a fool unable to understand anything of what you see, you will guess the bureaucrat by the fading of his sleeves, by that large horizontal stripe imprinted on his back by the chair on which he so often leans while pinching his pinch of snuff or resting from the strain of idleness. You will admire the businessman by the swelling of his pocket with its note-books; the *flanêur* by the sagging of his waistcoat pockets, where he often puts his hands; the shopkeeper by his extraordinarily open pockets, which are always gaping as if to complain about being deprived of their customary parcels. In short, a relatively clean, powdered, pomaded, worn-out collar; relatively frayed buttonholes; a sagging basque, the firmness of new buckram: these are the infallible diagnoses of professions, manners, and habits. There you have the fresh clothes of the dandy, the tweed of the person of independent means, the short frock coat of the second-rate broker, the sandy gold-buttoned tailcoat of the backward resident of Lyons, or a miser's grimy spencer.

Brummell was quite right to view CLOTHING as the culmination of elegant living; for it governs opinions, it determines them, it reigns! It is perhaps unfortunate, but that is the way of the world. Where fools abound, foolishness is perpetuated; and indeed, this thought should really be acknowledged as an axiom:

XLI

Negligence of clothing is moral suicide.

But if clothing is the whole man, it is even more so the whole woman. The slightest impropriety in a costume can relegate an unknown duchess to the lowest ranks of society.

While pondering over the set of grave questions of which the science of clothing consists, we were struck by the general nature of certain principles that govern, as it were, all countries, and the clothing of men as well as that of women; we then thought it necessary, in order to establish the laws of costume, to follow the very order in which we dress ourselves. And so certain facts prevail over the whole: for just as man dresses before speaking, before acting, he bathes before dressing. The divisions of this chapter thus result from conscientious observations, which have dictated the layout of the matter of dress as follows:

§ I. Ecumenical principles of clothing
§ II. On cleanliness in its relation to clothing
§ III. On the clothing of men
§ IV. On the clothing of women
§ V. On variations in costume, and summary of the chapter

People who dress like a laborer, whose bodies blithely don the same filthy and foul-smelling outward appearance every day, are as numerous as those simpletons who mix with high society and see nothing in it, who die without having lived, who recognize neither fine cuisine nor the true allure of women, who never utter a witticism or a foolish remark. But *my Lord, forgive them, for they know not what they do!*

If it is a question of converting them to elegance, will they ever comprehend these fundamental axioms of all our knowledge?

XLII

The boor covers himself, the rich man or the fool adorns himself, and the elegant man gets dressed.

XLIII

Clothing is at once a science, an art, a habit, and a sentiment.

Indeed, what forty-year-old woman does not recognize the profound science in clothing? You must admit that grace could not exist in an outfit if you were not accustomed to wearing it. Is there anything more ridiculous than a shopgirl in a court gown? And as for the sentiment of clothing, how many staunch believers will you reckon there are in society of women and men who are lavish with gold, fabrics, silks, the most wonderful creations of luxury, and who use them to make themselves look like Japanese idols! From this there follows an equally true aphorism, which even the most skilled coquettes and the professors of seduction should always closely observe:

XLIV

Clothing does not consist so much in clothes as in a certain manner of wearing them.

Consequently it is not the rags in themselves as it is the spirit of the rags that one must grasp. There exist a good number of people in the heart of the country, and even in Paris, capable of making, when it comes to new fashions, the same error as that Spanish duchess who, after receiving a precious basin of unknown form, believed, after lengthy meditation, that it was intended to appear on the table, and offered to her guests a casserole garnished with truffles, failing to realize the ideas of cleanliness essential to the gilded porcelain of that necessary piece of furniture.

These days our customs have so modified the costume that there is no longer, strictly speaking, any costume at all. Every European family has adopted woolen cloth, because the great lords, like the people, have instinctively understood this great truth: it is much better to wear broadcloth and to have horses than it is to litter an outfit with precious stones from the Middle Ages and the absolute monarchy. So, confined to clothing, elegance consists in an extreme refinement in the details of the outfit: it is less the simplicity of luxury than a luxurious simplicity. There is indeed another elegance; but it is only the vanity of clothing. It encourages certain women to wear bizarre fabrics just to be noticed, to use diamond fasteners to tie a knot; to put a sparkling loop into the bow of a ribbon; in the same way that certain martyrs of fashion, people with a hundred louis income, who live in a garret and want *to be seen in the latest style*, have stones on their shirt in the morning, fasten their pants with golden buttons, hold their lorgnettes by chains, and go to dine at Tabar's! . . .[53] How many of these Parisian Tantaluses are unaware of, perhaps deliberately ignore, this axiom:

XLV

Clothing must never be a luxury.

Many people, even among those whom we have acknowledged have some distinction in ideas, education, and superiority of the heart, have trouble knowing the borderline separating walking clothes from riding clothes!

What an ineffable pleasure for the observer, for the connoisseur, to encounter on the streets of Paris, along the boulevards, those women of genius who, after having written their name, their rank, and their fortune in their feeling for their clothing, appear as nothing to the eyes of the common herd but are an absolute poem for artists, for society people out strolling! It is a perfect harmony between the color of the outfit and that of drawings; it is the finesse of the charms that reveals the industrious hand of a skillful chambermaid. These high feminine powers know wonderfully well how to conform to the humble role of pedestrian, for they have so often experienced the audacities authorized by an equipage; for it is only those accustomed to the luxury of the coach who know how to get dressed to go on foot.

It is to one of those ravishing Parisian goddesses whom we owe the two following formulas:

XLVI

The equipage is a passport to anything that a woman wishes to dare.

XLVII

The foot soldier has always to fight against a prejudice.

From which it follows that the following axiom must, above all, regulate the clothing of prosaic pedestrians:

XLVIII

Anything that aims at an effect is in bad taste, as is anything that is tumultuous.

Brummell has, moreover, left us a most admirable maxim on this matter, and England's approval has consecrated it:

XLIX

If people look at you closely, you are not well attired: you are too well attired, too stiff, or too mannered.

According to this immortal sentence, every foot soldier should pass unnoticed. His triumph is to be at once vulgar and refined, recognized by his own and ignored by the mob. If Murat was nicknamed King Franconi,[54] judge the severity with which the world pursues a smug man! He falls beneath ridicule. Excessive refinement is perhaps a greater vice than lack of care, and the following axiom shall probably make pretentious women tremble:

L

To go beyond the limits of fashion is to become a caricature.

It now remains for us to destroy the gravest of all the errors that a false experiment substantiates among minds unaccustomed to thinking or observing; but we shall give our sovereign ruling despotically and without comment, leaving to women of good taste and to the philosophers of the salon the care of discussing it:

LI

An article of clothing is like a coat of paint; it sets everything in relief, and clothing was invented more to make corporal advantages stand out than to hide imperfections.

From which follows this natural corollary:

LII

Anything that an outfit seeks to hide, conceal, augment, and exaggerate more than nature or fashion prescribes or requires, is always presumed to be licentious.

Consequently, any fashion that has a lie as its objective is essentially transient and in bad taste.

By these principles, derived from an accurate precedent, based on observation, and stemming from the severest human or feminine pride, it is clear that an unattractive, misshapen, hunchbacked, or lame woman must try, out of politeness, to diminish her failings; but she would be less than a woman if she imagined herself to be producing the slightest illusion. Mademoiselle de la Vallière[55] limped gracefully, and more than one hunchback has known how to take their revenge through a charming spirit or the dazzling riches of a passionate heart. When shall women understand that a failing gives them tremendous advantages! . . . Perfect men or women are the most useless creatures.

We shall conclude these preliminary reflections, applicable to every country, with an axiom that needs no comment:

LIII

A rip is a misfortune, a stain is a vice.

....

OCTOBER–NOVEMBER 1830.

NOTES

1. Charles Dupin (1784–1873), a political economist, had invented the choroplethmap a few years earlier in 1826—a map in which areas (countries, states, etc.) are shaded or colored to reflect corresponding data. (The name "choroplethmap" would not be given to it until 1938.)

2. The rue Boucherat used to form part of what is now the rue de Turenne in the Marais district in Paris.

3. The Saint Denis Abbey educated members of the Legion of Honor.

4. *Cité dolente*: from the words over the gate to Dante's hell. See the opening verse to Canto III of the *Inferno*: "Per me si va ne la città dolente."

5. *Chiens de cour*: what students used to call the house masters in charge of watching over them in the schoolyard in Balzac's time.

6. The baron Antoine Portal (1742–1843) was doctor to Louis XVIII. He created the Royal Academy of Medicine in 1820. He presumably did not ride about in style.

7. The Théâtre Feydeau closed its doors on 16 April 1829, a year before Balzac was writing this, making the attainment of a box seat even more of an empty accomplishment.

8. A *britschka* (the German form; also *britzka* or *brichka*) was a long four-wheeled carriage with a folding top over the rear seat and a rear-facing front seat. It was generally pulled by two, not four, horses.

9. Sir Robert Peel (1788–1850) was Home Secretary and had introduced reforms into British criminal law when Balzac had written this. A few years later, Peel would serve the first of two terms as Conservative Prime Minister of the United Kingdom. François-Auguste-René, viscount de Chateaubriand (1768–1848), was founder of Romanticism in France. In the realm of elegant living, though, he was also known for giving his name to a cut of tenderloin.

10. Émile de Girardin (1802–1881), journalist and founder of *La Mode*, in which Balzac's *Treatise* was first published.

11. Rose Fortassier, in her notes to the Pléiade edition of this text, proposes that Balzac is here referring to *Adam* Smith, although such a citation would be a tad perverse. *An Inquiry into the Nature and Causes of the Wealth of Nations*, which was well known in France at this time, would have set elegant living as the end result of human labor.

12. Joseph Jacotot (1770–1840), exiled during the Second Restoration, had just been allowed to return to France when Balzac was writing this, owing to the Revolution of 1830. Author of the method of "intellectual emancipation" (or the "panecastic method"), Jacotot remains a very interesting figure in the history of pedagogy. When appointed professor of French langauge at the University of Louvain in 1818, knowing no Flemish or Dutch, and his students no French, Jacotot overcame this obstacle by giving his students dual language selections of Fénélon's *Adventures of Telemachus* with the idea that thorough knowledge of a microcosm of French literature would lead to a knowledge of the macrocosm. The resulting success led to his establishing three essential principles: 1. All men have equal intelligence, and differ only in their will to use it; 2. Every man has received from God the faculty of being able to instruct himself; and 3. Everything is in everything. Thus, by

knowing one thing well (in the cited case, Fénélon's *Telemachus*), one can then refer everything else (elegant living, for example) back to it.

Salente is the ideal city in *Telemachus* overseen by the character of Mentor. The Constitution takes a pretty hard stand on elegant living as Balzac describes it.

13. Victor Cousin (1792–1867), philosopher, popularized the work of Kant and Hegel, and founded the school of Eclecticism. The work Balzac cites appeared in 1827.

14. Émile Chodruc-Duclos (1780–1842), humanist and ultra-Royalist, was known at the time for wandering about in rags, and was referred to as the "Diogenes of the Palais Royale."

15. The Napoleonic code was adopted as French civil law in 1804; two months later Napoléon Bonaparte was proclaimed French emperor. The year 1120 is when Louis VI of France agreed to terms of peace with Henry I after suffering a humiliating defeat against his forces.

16. Auguste Ravez (1770–1849) had been President of the Chamber of Deputies of the Departments from 11 December 1818 to 5 November 1827.

17. A "centaur" would refer to those with a strong penchant for riding horses. Dandies would often refer to themselves, or be referred to, as such, and riding outfits were essential components to elegant dress.

18. Solon (638 BC–559 BC), lawmaker of Athens and lyric poet. Balzac is perhaps "updating" one of Solon's better-known statements: "Put more trust in the nobility of character than in an oath."

19. Red heels (*Talons rouges*) were a style introduced among the nobility through imitation of Louis XIV. Such decorative attention to what is normally the most utilitarian portion of an outfit made for an immediate sign for idleness.

20. Catherine and Marie de Médicis.

21. Anne and Marie-Thérèse of Austria.

22. Benvenuto Cellini (1500–1571) was an Italian Renaissance goldsmith, painter, sculptor, soldier, and musician. The saltcellar in question was made for Francis I. It was stolen from the Kunsthistorisches Museum in Vienna in 2003 and recovered in 2006.

23. François Barrière (1786–1868) had just published *Tableaux de génie et d'histoire* in 1828, and *La Cour et la ville sous Louis XIV, Louis XV et Louis XVI* in 1829.

24. The reactionary Jean-François Joly de Fleury (1718–1802) was briefly financial minister after Jacques Necker resigned in 1781. He tried to undo some of the changes that had preceded him, such as the abolition of the royal corvée.

25. I.e., a record of one's noble lineage.

26. *Elle est le principe des œuvres comme des ouvrages.*

27. A *"tigre"* was a "fashionable" term for a groom of small stature.

28. Charles Latour-Mézeray, owner and editor of the *Journal des Enfans*, was also known as "the Man with the Camellia," as he would always wear a white one in his buttonhole.

29. *L'Organisateur* was the first Saint-Simonian paper, founded in 1819.

30. Richard Brinsley Sheridan (1751–1816), Irish playwright and Whig Statesman, is best remembered for his play *The School for Scandal.* He served in Parliament from 1780 until 1812. Drinking and womanizing were two of his better-known vices.

31. Elizabeth Conyngham (1769–1861) was the last mistress of George IV.

32. *Ambo pares*: "both equal."

33. Brummell's companion in exile was in fact Berkeley Craven, not William Craddock.

34. Father Gaultier (1745–1818) was author of *Traits caractéristiques d'une mauvaise éducation ou Actions et discours contraires à la politesse* (Characteristic traits of a bad education or actions and speech contrary to courtesy) (1796).

35. See *Tristam Shandy* v. IX, ch. XIII: "'—I maintain it, the conceits of a rough-bearded man are seven years more terse and juvenile for one single operation; and if they did not run a risk of being quite shaved away, might be carried up by continual shavings to the highest pitch of sublimity—How Homer could write with so long a beard, I don't know—'"

36. This planned chapter became the essay *Théorie de la démarche.*

37. Joseph Marie Eugène Sue (1804–1857), best remembered for the sprawling serial novels *The Mysteries of Paris* and *The Wandering Jew*, was a dandy of particular interest in that he was also a Socialist.

38. Georges Cuvier (1769–1832), French naturalist and zoologist, established the fields of comparative anatomy and paleontology. His ability to reconstruct a living animal from a fossil made him something of a supreme physiologist for Balzac. His methods of relating part to whole also make him a comparable figure to Joseph Jacotot, mentioned earlier.

39. David d'Angers (1788–1856), French sculptor. Among his works are a number of sculptures for tombs in the Père Lachaise Cemetery,

including a bronze bust of Balzac. Jean-Pierre Cortot (1787–1843) was also a French sculptor.

40. Amable Tastu (1798–1885) was a French writer and poet, no longer famous, but remembered for being the author of librettos for such musicians as Saint-Saëns.

41. Mattieu Laensberg was an astrologer who put out a popular series of almanacs predicting events and weather.

42. Bernard de Bovier de Fontenelle (1657–1757) was the author of the 1686 *Conversations on the Plurality of Worlds*, a foundational work of the Enlightenment that described a heliocentric model of the universe. Immanuel Kant quoted him in his *Critique of Practical Reason*: "I bow before a great man, but my spirit does not bow."

43. The Hôtel Dessein was a fashionable hotel in Calais, memorialized in Laurence Sterne's *A Sentimental Journey through France and Italy* (in which the hotel-keeper Dessein makes an appearance in a number of chapters) and William Makepeace Thackery's *Roundabout Papers*. It was Beau Brummell's first stop when he went into exile.

44. Laure Pernon Junot (1784–1838), the Duchesse d'Abrantès (nicknamed the Duchesse d'Abracadabrantès by Théophile Gauthier) had known Napoléon throughout his life, was the author of fifty-seven volumes of memoirs, and was known for being in her day one of the most beautiful women of the imperial court. She had become Balzac's mistress a couple of years earlier and he had played a large part in the writing of her *Memoirs*.

45. François de Bassompierre (1579–1646), French courtier, was a favorite of King Henry IV and was later Marshal of France.

46. Constantin Abraham (1785–1855) specialized in painting on porcelain. *La fornarina* (the "Bakeress," but also known as *Portrait of a Young Woman*) was painted by Raphael sometime between 1518 and 1520.

47. Charles Maurice de Talleyrand-Périgord, Prince de Benevente (1754–1838), known more simply as Talleyrand, the "Prince of Diplomats," was the first Prime Minister of France. The quote Balzac is referring to is "Speech is a faculty given to man to conceal his thoughts."

48. Balzac's use of the English word "pocket" refers to a "pocket book," or a pocket dictionary.

49. Charles Nodier, French writer and noteworthy librarian, was a crucial figure in French Romanticism, but lesser known than those he influenced, such as Victor Hugo and Alfred de Musset. His portrait of the Colonel Oudet had recently appeared when Balzac was writing this; it would shortly be collected in the second volume of Nodier's *Souvenirs, épisodes et portraits pour servir à l'histoire de la révolution et de l'empire* (1831).

General Oudet was the head of the secret society of the "Philadelphians," a Republican conspiracy against Napoléon. He perished under mysterious circumstances in the Battle of Wagram.

50. Hippolyte Auger (1796–1881), French dramatist, worked on many of the same journals as Balzac at this time, including *Le Silhouette* and the *Feuilleton des Journaux Politiques.*

51. The "titus" was a hairstyle made popular by the French Revolution: short, upswept hair, exposing the neck and evoking the haircuts given to prisoners by their executioners before being guillotined.

52. Franz Joseph Gall (1758–1828) was the inventor of "Cranioscopy" (what would later be renamed "phrenology"): the determination of intellectual faculties based on the shape of the skull. Johann Caspar

Lavater (1741–1801), a Swiss poet and antagonist of rationalism, is best remembered for his work on physiognomy.

53. Tabar's was a famous restaurant during the Restoration period.

54. Joachim Murat (1767–1815), brother-in-law of Napoléon Bonaparte, was nicknamed "King Franconi" by the latter after a famous circus rider owing to his flamboyant clothes. Other nicknames included "The Abbot with the Beautiful Leg" and "The Handsome Swordsman." He was, for all that, equally respected for his bravery.

55. Louise François de La Baume Le Blanc, or Louise de La Vallière (1644–1710), was one of Louis XIV's mistresses (and according to Sainte-Beuve, the most interesting of them). She apparently limped, owing to a sprained ankle in her youth.

WAKEFIELD HANDBOOKS

1. *Treatise on Elegant Living*, Honoré de Balzac

2. *The Young Girl's Handbook of Good Manners for Use in Educational Establishments*, Pierre Louÿs